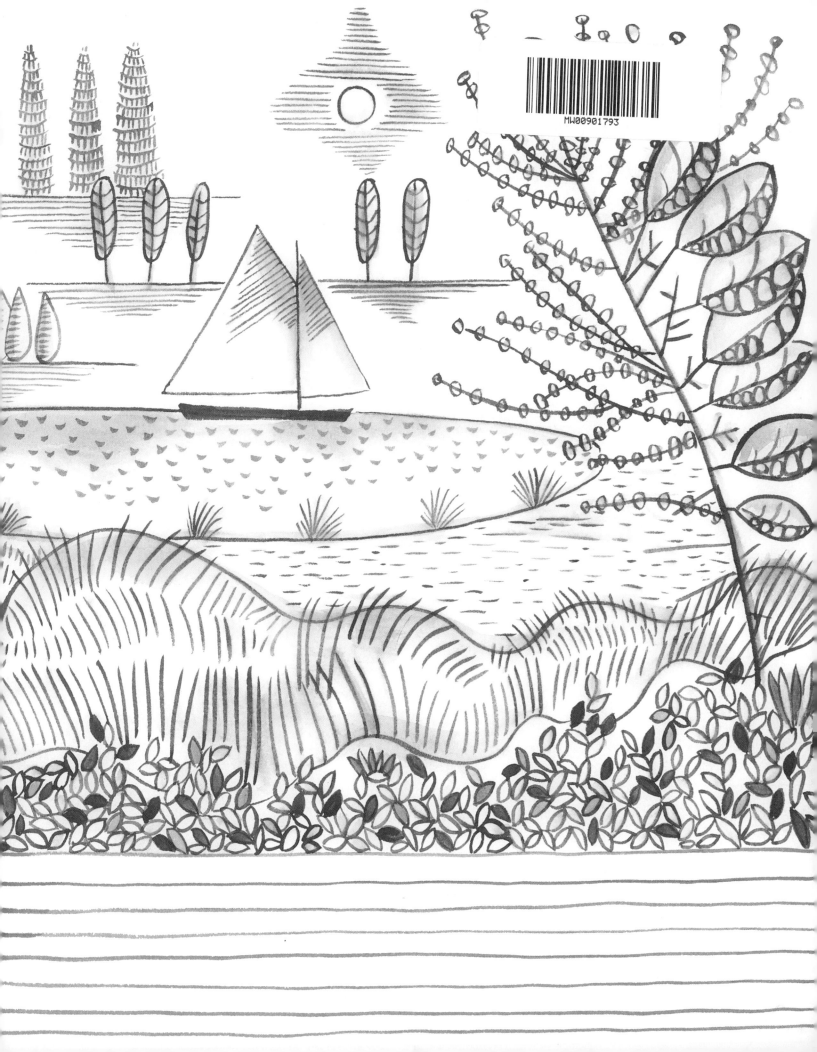

With love to the main characters in my life. —L. B.

Library of Congress Cataloging-in-Publication Data available.

ISBN 978-1-4521-5529-6

Manufactured in China.

Design by Sara Gillingham Studio.
Typeset in Quimbly.
The illustrations in this book were rendered in gouache.

10 9 8 7 6 5 4 3 2 1

Chronicle Books LLC
680 Second Street
San Francisco, California 94107

Chronicle Books—we see things differently.
Become part of our community at www.chroniclekids.com.

NIGHT PLAY

A Bedtime Story in Three Acts

Lizi Boyd

chronicle books · san francisco

ACT 2 FRIENDS WIDE AWAKE

For Act 2,
we need . . .

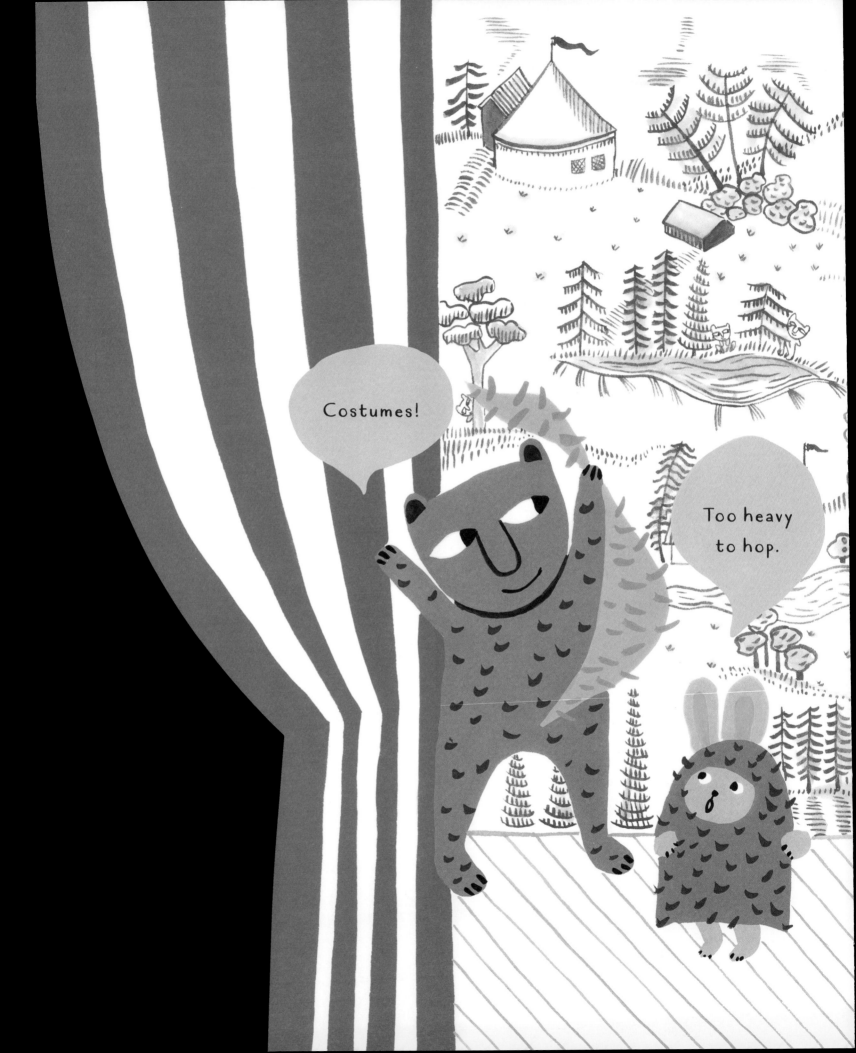

ACT 3 ALL SAIL

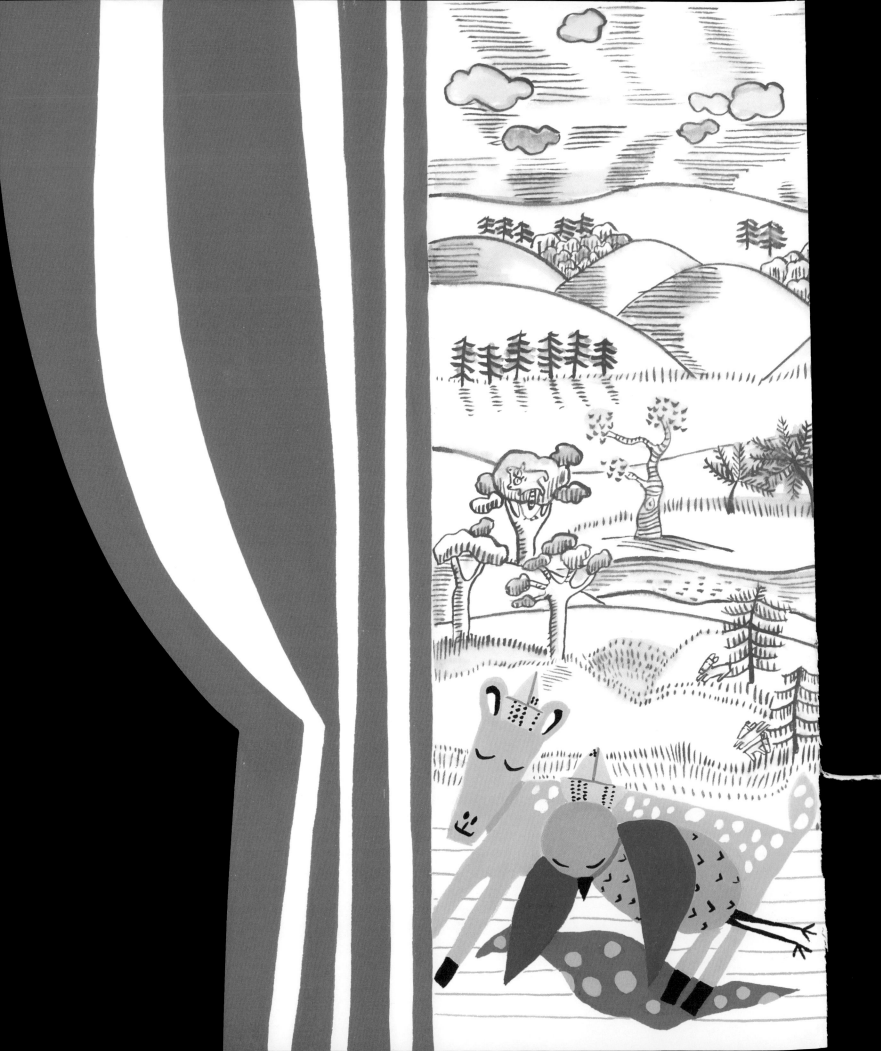